Out of Office

ANNAH CONWELL

D1519658

To everyone who wanted Brad and Zara to get together. Thank you for caring about my characters. This one's for you!

But when it comes down to it I just want to be near you.

– Don't Make Me Wait, Johnnyswim

Contents

CHAPTER 1

Zara Thomas

"Young love is so beautiful." I sigh happily as I regard the couple embracing across the office. I rest my chin on my arms, which are propped up on the top of my low cubicle wall.

"You're younger than them, and they've been together for over a year now," Brad, my coworker and cubicle neighbor, points out.

I roll my eyes. "It's still beautiful." Our mutual friends Charlotte and Callum are getting married this December, and since we all work together at Wreston Bank, we get to see them be all lovey-dovey every day. A few people have complained, but not me. I've been told I'm too much of a romantic, but I can't help it. There's something about a good love story that turns me into a happy puddle. Can puddles be happy? I'm going to go with yes.

"It's nice," Brad remarks, drawing my attention back to him. Brad is the senior software engineer on our team. He's got on his signature wardrobe piece: cargo shorts. Yes, it's November. No, that did not stop him from wearing them to work today. He just opted for a hoodie instead of his usual polo or T-shirt. So even though he's eight years older than me, his wardrobe is that of a middle school boy.

There have been a few times over the past year—mostly when he wears something other than those awful shorts—that I've found him attractive, but I brush the feeling away quickly. Our age gap makes things awkward at times with him being in his thirties and me in my twenties. Plus his position being over mine creates this odd power dynamic that I'm not sure we could get past.

Charlotte and Callum have managed to make an office relationship work, but I watched them go through the wringer for it, and they didn't even have an awkward age gap acting as a wedge. They're all the better because of it, but I don't know that it would work out that way for us.

"I can't believe there are people in the office who don't like them. It's not like they go overboard with the PDA. And Charlotte is the nicest human in this whole building," I say.

Brad shrugs. "Not everyone thinks office romances are appropriate." He turns back toward his computer screen, lines of code covering the black background. "I'm assuming you think they're fine, based on your reaction to Charlotte and Callum."

I raise my eyebrows at his question. He types on his keyboard in a seemingly nonchalant manner. He's not...*fishing*, is he? Surely not.

"I don't think they're inappropriate," I say, studying the back of his head. His sandy blond hair is the length that's too long to be short and too short to be long—that medium length no one knows what to call. And his shoulders are broad, but his hoodie conceals whether they're muscular or not. The man is an enigma. "What do you think of them?"

His typing pauses. "I think under the right circumstances, they're appropriate."

"And what might those circumstances be?" The words come out before I can think about how they sound. This annoying habit of mine tends to get me in trouble. Now I'm toeing the line of flirting with a guy who is supposed to be my superior. *Nice, Zara, way to make things awkward.*

He swivels his chair toward me, leveling his powder blue eyes on me. "Mutual desire," he pauses, and I swear his voice sounds gruffer than usual. "A solid friendship. Maturity."

"You sound like you have experience with office romance," I say, again without thinking. There's a chance I won't ever learn how to hold my tongue.

"Not exactly." He turns back to his computer monitor and I scrunch my brows together. *Not exactly? What does that mean?* I'm about to reprimand him for being cryptic when Callum appears by our cubicle cluster.

"Morning meeting in my office," Callum says in his usual blunt way, but his smile softens the statement. Before Charlotte, he was a man of few smiles. Now, her sunshine is rubbing off on him.

"Love looks good on you, boss," I say, and he gives me a dark look. I've made him double annoyed today with my comment on his love life and use of his least favorite nickname: boss. Thankfully, I'm too good at my job and too close to his future wife to be fired for my button-pushing ways.

"You're lucky Charlotte likes you," he grumbles, then stalks off to his office. I laugh and snag my laptop up off my desk in case I need it during the meeting.

"You enjoy messing with him too much." Brad laughs, making my smile widen.

"It is an entertaining pastime."

He chuckles and leaves his cubicle while I tuck my laptop under my arm. I watch him walk, curiosity tugging at my mind like a cat with a ball of yarn. I've never thought of Brad as much more than an attractive friend, but his words from earlier have me wondering what could be hiding underneath his casual appearance and easygoing smile. I wave off the thoughts my hopeless romantic heart attempts to conjure up. There are plenty of reasons not to think of Brad as more than a friend I work with. I don't need to get caught up in the idea of him pining after me.

Not that he *would* pine after me. I'm sure I can't be his type being so young and not as far along in my career as him. And while I don't think I'm immature, I'm not as mature as the women his age most likely are. Not to mention I have blue hair, which could be a turn-off for him. Either way, it wouldn't do me any good to entertain that fantasy, because I don't even really like him like that. So it's settled. I don't like him, and I won't secretly fantasize over the idea of him being in love with me. That's an easy fix.

I walk into Callum's office and Brad looks over at me, smiling.

He does have a nice smile...

CHAPTER 2

Brad Jennings

My palms are sweating so profusely that I have to rub them down my cargo shorts to dry them. Why did I think it was a good idea to try flirting–with *Zara* no less? I'm not a stranger to the dating scene, but I'm also no Casanova. And when it comes to Zara, any attempt at more than friendly conversation seems to leave me out of breath and perspiring. She's an intimidating woman with her bright hair, sassy attitude, and intelligence in the office. I've worked with quite a few junior software engineers in my day, and she's one of the best.

I could be biased, considering I find her to also be drop-dead gorgeous, but Callum wouldn't have hired her if he didn't think she was capable. And he definitely wouldn't have kept her on if she didn't exceed expectations. All in all, the woman is downright perfect, and I'm struggling to climb out of the friend abyss she has thrown me into. I say abyss instead of zone because an abyss is much more difficult to get out of.

"Brad?" Callum's voice pulls my wayward train of thought back onto the rails.

"Yes?" I look at him. His eyebrows are raised and he's leaning back in his chair, clearly waiting for me to answer a question I never heard him ask.

"I asked for an update on the mobile check deposit feature."

"Right." I clear my throat. "It's in the testing stage now, and we're addressing bugs as they come up."

"When do you anticipate it being in production?"

"I think by the end of the year is a reasonable expectation."

He nods at my answer, then claps his hands together once. "Alright, I'll let you two get back to work." I stand up, ready to leave at his dismissal. "Make sure you both are documenting your work as you go for audit." He grinds out the last word. Even though his own fiancé is on the auditing team, he still hates that department.

"You got it, boss!" Zara chirps, flicking two fingers away from her forehead in a half-salute. Callum scowls while I laugh. As Zara turns to leave, our eyes catch. Her irises are like pools of dark chocolate, rich and deep. She averts her gaze quickly, tucking a dark blue strand behind her ear and breezing past me.

I follow behind her and–I'm not proud of this–I check her out. Just a *little*. It's almost impossible not to, really. She's got on black sweatpants, a fitted white top, and white platform tennis shoes. Zara and I both take advantage of the lack of a dress code at Wreston but in different ways. She manages to look like some sort of fitness model most days, while I look, well, functional, I suppose.

I don't think I have a style, per se. I just wear what's comfortable and practical. My cargo shorts have pockets for all my stuff, and they're worn in enough to be comfortable while sitting at a desk all day. I briefly consider that my fashion choices are keeping me in the friend abyss with Zara, but she has worn *Sesame Street* pajamas to work before, saying she slept in. So the style factor can't be so important to her.

I sink into my office chair, determined to get some focused work done. I thought Zara was beautiful when I first met her, but after spending so much time with her talking about Charlotte and Callum, I've started to care for her as more than a coworker. And that shift has made it difficult to focus when she's right next to me. She's practically magnetic by nature.

Her soft humming comes over the short cubicle wall between us. I listen closely and notice she's humming *Rudolph the Red-Nosed Reindeer*, which makes me smile.

"You must be a Christmas-before-Thanksgiving person," I say, and her humming ceases.

"I am," she says with a light laugh. "There's no reason to wait to celebrate the best holiday."

I stand and look over the cubicle wall to find her scrolling through her inbox. "I agree," I say, and she turns her head to gift me with her smile. "Is Rudolph one of your favorites?" I ask, hoping to keep our conversation going.

"I love too many Christmas movies to pick a favorite, but it is a top contender. Except not the Claymation one." She shivers dramatically. "That one should be a Halloween movie instead with how creepy it is."

"*Claymation Rudolph* is a classic!" I say, and she rolls her eyes.

"That's what people always say. Just because something is old doesn't make it a classic."

"When did you last watch it?"

"I think I was five? I didn't sleep for a week afterward." She wrinkles her nose, making me laugh.

"That's your problem, then. You need to see it under the right circumstances as an adult."

"And what might those circumstances be?" A teasing smile is on her lips, and I recall our conversation before the meeting when she was asking about office romances. My palms are already getting warm. I'm in unchartered territory again. *Is she flirting?*

"Homemade hot cocoa, lots of blankets, and a person who loves the movie to point out the best parts." I rattle off the initial things that come to mind. Hopefully, I don't sound as awkward as I'm starting to feel.

"That does sound nice," she says with a soft smile. "But I think I'd rather watch the animated version under those same circumstances."

"You could always do a double feature."

"I might have to try that." *With me.* The words shine like a Vegas billboard in my mind, but they never leave my lips. I thought I was setting her up for an easy acceptance of my subtle invitation, but either I'm really bad at flirting or she's bad at taking hints.

Or she doesn't want to date you.

The thought forms a pit in my stomach.

CHAPTER 3

Zara Thomas

"Zara!" I jump at the sound of my name being squealed at a decibel a touch too high for the workplace. I whip my head to the right to see Charlotte peeking over my cubicle wall, dangling a pink envelope over the edge.

"Hey, Lottie," I say, using the nickname that most of her friends call her. "What's this?" I take the envelope from her hand. She walks around the gray office wall and into my small space.

"It's your invitation to the bachelorette party!" She gestures to the envelope like it's a game show prize, her sparkly mauve fingernails glimmering in the light. I grin up at her from my desk chair and rip open the envelope. Lottie doesn't do anything halfway, so I'm anticipating something amazing for her bachelorette party.

The invitation is a rose pink with gold glitter trim that dusts my black sweatpants upon touching it. When I open it, something resembling a gift certificate falls into my lap. I pick it up and read.

"A spa day?" I couldn't hide the excitement from my voice even if I wanted to.

"Yes! A day of pampering followed by getting ready to go out with the boys. We'll take a limo to a country dance hall to cap off the night!" Leave it to Charlotte to plan out an entire day instead of just one party.

"This sounds amazing, Lottie!" I stand up and hug her. "Thank you for including me in your wedding."

She squeezes me tight. "You're one of my closest friends! I couldn't have my big day without you up there with me."

"Well, it's an honor," I say with a smile as we pull apart.

"This is all so exciting!" she trills. "I have to go back to work, but I couldn't wait any longer to give this to you." She hugs me once more, then speeds off in a blur of pink, her signature color.

I smile to myself as I search for a pushpin to stick on the small corkboard that decorates my office space. It's difficult to make a cubicle feel homey, but I've done my best with photos and memories pinned up and some fake plants near my monitors. There's also the blue rubber duck that Lottie gifted me last year. I have him on an upside-down ramekin as a pedestal.

After retrieving the pushpin, I turn to put up the sparkly invitation. Right as I'm adjusting it, though, a voice startles me for the second time today.

"New addition to the corkboard? Must be important," Brad says. I prick my finger upon his surprise, and a spot of blood appears. Careful not to get blood on the card, I finish pinning it up before turning to address him.

"It's just the invitation for the bachelorette party. I think it will liven up the bland walls of this place," I say, then press my fingertip in between my lips to try to stop the bleeding. Brad's eyes travel to my mouth then back, and I swear there's heat in those blue eyes of his.

"Did you hurt yourself?" he asks, dipping his head toward where I'm now holding my finger out in front of me.

I lift my hand to show him. "Just pricked it is all."

"I've got some Band-Aids in my desk drawer. Don't want you to get blood on your keyboard." He disappears for a moment, ducking down, then reappears at the entrance to my cubicle. Stepping inside he holds his hand out, but there's no Band-Aid visible.

I tilt my head, perplexed. Upon seeing my confusion, he reveals that the Band-Aid is in his other hand.

"Allow me," he says with a gesture toward my injured hand. Befuddled by his request, I set my hand, palm side up, in his own. I'm surprised by the warmth that floods my body upon contact. Brad carefully wraps the Band-Aid around the tip of my finger, and I flick my gaze from his face to his gentle hands as he works.

When he's done, he runs his thumb over my palm to the inside of my wrist, making tingles flow down my spine. I tug my hand away, surprised by the sudden reaction within me.

"Thank you," I breathe out.

"Anytime," he says, his own voice barely above a whisper. He turns away and walks out of my cubicle, not going into his own but heading toward the elevators instead.

I plop down into my office chair, dazed. I have never felt that way around Brad. To be honest, I haven't felt that way around many people at all. In college, most of the guys I met didn't take me seriously due to my colorful hair and male-dominated major. So, that led me to a string of disappointing dates, then a hiatus from relationships altogether.

Am I so attention-starved that I'm reading into moments with Brad? Surely that must be it. I highly doubt the man is into me. And I can't be into him, either. Maybe he put on one of those pheromone colognes and it's set me into some weird hormonal frenzy. Anything has to be more logical than this.

I try to shake off my thoughts and get some coding done, but every time my pricked fingertip brushes the keyboard, I think of his gentle touch and heated gaze.

What is wrong with me?

CHAPTER 4

Brad Jennings

What is wrong with me?

I barrel through the lobby doors and out into the chilly November air. What was I thinking stroking her hand like that? From the way she jerked it back, I wouldn't be surprised if I returned to find an HR representative waiting on me. I thought I was reading the situation clearly, but now I feel like an idiot.

I scrub my hands down my face as I pace away from the building. She's never even hinted at any sort of attraction to me and here I go stroking her wrist after giving her a Band-Aid like some weird vampire from a teen movie.

The wind bites at my face and legs. I walk back inside and let the warm lobby air thaw my skin.

A woman enters after me and directs a concerned look toward my cargo shorts. I avoid her disapproving eyebrow raise and look down at my sneakers. At least I'm not wearing flip-flops.

"Brad?" Charlotte's voice makes me lift my head. She says something to the group of suit-clad men she's standing with before walking toward me.

"Hey, Charlotte," I say with a nod. Here's to hoping I look casual and not like a madman pacing the streets outside of our office.

"Hey, everything alright? You look a little...stressed," she says and tilts her head to the side.

"I'm all good!" I say quickly, making her eyes widen a little. Came on a little strong there, I guess. "I just needed some air is all. And now I feel great." I don't enjoy lying to my friends, but this one slipped out. I feel the opposite of great.

"Okay," she drags out the last syllable, looking at me like I've lost my mind. Though I haven't lost it. I've just handed it and my heart to the pretty girl in the cubicle next to mine. Charlotte can't know this, though, because she would try to meddle. And while Zara and I definitely meddled in her and Callum's relationship, I don't want her in ours. The irony is not lost on me.

"I should get back to my desk." I shift back and forth on my feet.

She nods. "I've got a meeting to get to. But how does lunch sound? You and Zara with Callum and me?" My abdomen tightens with a mixture of dread and excitement.

"Sounds great!" I force a smile onto my face and wave her goodbye before dragging my feet to the elevator. Here's hoping Zara doesn't think I'm a total freak for what I did earlier.

After returning to my desk, I spend the morning in awkward silence. I try to work, but time and time again I wonder what Zara is doing, thinking, and feeling. She's a distraction in more ways than one.

Now it's time to go to lunch, and I feel unprepared. Charlotte and Callum said they'd meet us at a local burger place after their respective meetings, so I'm likely going to have to walk to the restaurant with Zara...alone.

Sure enough, as soon as I push in my desk chair, Zara walks past my cubicle. I walk out behind her and follow her to the elevators. She presses the button and I come to stand beside her, waiting for the elevator to reach our floor.

"Hey," I rasp out, then clear my throat.

"Hey," she says back. I open my mouth to say something when the elevator doors slide open with a ding.

She steps on first and I follow, then press the button for the ground floor. After we've gone down a few floors I'm feeling fidgety and frustrated. Things between Zara and me have never been this way. This is exactly what I wanted to avoid. I shouldn't have pushed the boundary between us.

Zara clears her throat, making me snap my head toward her. "I bought the Claymation Rudolph last night." She bites her lip, and it takes every ounce of control in me not to stare at her mouth when she does.

"You did? What did you think?"

"I ordered the DVD off Amazon, so I haven't watched it yet. I know my generation is all about downloading everything, but I like to have phys- ical copies of movies–especially Christmas ones." An uncomfortable feeling settles in my stomach whenever she talks about 'her generation.' I know there's a gap between us, but it doesn't seem that large until it's brought up like this.

"You'll have to let me know what you think when- ever you do watch it." I turn my head and watch the elevator numbers get lower and lower.

"I will! Though it might take me a little while to get to it."

"Why's that?" I ask, eyes still ahead instead of on her. Less risky.

"I think it's best to watch older Christmas movies with someone. Cuddled up under a blanket, lights twinkling, things like that. But it has to be the right person, like you said before. Someone who loves the movie." My heart picks up speed and my mouth goes dry. I look over at her right as the elevator doors open once again. I try to decipher her expression, but it's under lock and key as she leaves the elevator. I stand there for a moment, stunned.

Maybe pushing this friendship boundary isn't so bad after all.

CHAPTER 5

Zara Thomas

They're not here. Charlotte and Callum have bailed on us, which means I am now alone with Brad. I stare at the group text Charlotte sent with a frown.

Lottie: Hey, something came up last minute and we can't make it. I'm SO sorry! We'd be there if we could. I hope y'all can still have a good time!

Whatever came up must be important because Charlotte rarely bails on friends. She's loyal to a fault. Worry pricks at my conscious and I open a private message with just her.

Zara: Hey Lottie, everything okay?

Lottie: Yes! Our caterer just cancelled on us last minute so we're headed to meet one that has an opening for our date.

"Do you still want to get lunch?" Brad asks, and I lock my phone before sliding it into the black crossbody bag slung over my shoulder.

"Might as well since we're already here." I shrug. We walk up to the counter to order, and I make sure that I pay fast before Brad gets any ideas. Not that he would. *Just because he gave you a Band-Aid doesn't mean he likes you enough to buy you lunch.* I should tell myself that over and over, especially since I accidentally flirted with him in the elevator.

I sigh as I step away from the counter to wait on him. Why, oh why, did I insinuate I wanted to watch a movie with him? I watch from nearby as he digs out a brown leather wallet from his cargo shorts. It's a surprisingly nice wallet considering the casual nature of his outfit. It would be such a bad idea to cross that line with him, even if I did like him. Which I don't. Because we don't have anything in common besides work and our two best friends. And he wears cargo shorts.

Though, if anyone could make them look cute, it's Brad... *No.* I need to stay strong. If I don't, I'll fly off into a magical fantasy land where I make myself believe he's in love with me and I end up brokenhearted without a job. Every girl knows not to date her superior in the corporate world. It's hard enough being a woman in tech, much less having everyone think you're trying to sleep your way to the top. Never mind the fact that there would be no–ahem– *sleeping* until marriage. People always see what they want to. Normally I don't mind, but job security is important to me. I don't love Wreston, but I do love my job. I also love being able to eat and pay bills.

Brad grabs his table number and foam cup from the cashier and turns toward me. I turn on my heel to disguise the fact that I was watching him, only to run straight into a tall, scowling businessman.

"Watch it!" The man grunts and shoves past me. He stalks out the door at high speed, probably on his way to fire someone for not making his cappuccino just right.

"Are you okay?" Brad asks and runs a hand over my upper arm. I tilt my head and look up, meeting his eyes. It's rare that we're ever this close to one another. I've never noticed how blue his eyes are, like a perfectly worn-in pale denim jacket. The kind you snuggle up in by a fire while the air smells of cinnamon and pine. It takes me a minute to remember he asked me a question.

"I'm okay," I breathe out.

"If that guy wouldn't have stormed out of here so fast, he'd be giving you an apology right now," he says, his jaw tight and brows furrowed. Heat rushes through me at the protective glare he's wearing. His hand is still holding my upper arm, the light grip sending tingles down my arm to my fingertips.

"It was my fault. I ran into him."

Brad shakes his head at my words. "People always deserve to be treated with respect."

The butterflies in my stomach settle down. This wasn't about me. He would have done this for anyone. Which is good, because there's nothing between us anyway. I step back, pulling my arm from his grip. I'm not sure why I feel cold all of a sudden, as if his touch had any effect on me.

"Yes, well, it's no big deal!" I paste on a smile. "He's gone now. We should have lunch before our break is up," I say and turn toward the fountain drink dispenser. I fill my cup with ice cubes, followed by Dr Pepper.

"I'm kind of glad Callum isn't here. He would make fun of us for our soda choice," Brad says from behind me, making me glance over my shoulder. His usual easygoing smile replaces his glare from earlier. Ignoring the warmth that arises at the sight, I press a plastic lid on top of my cup.

"Ugh, yes. Just because he doesn't drink soda doesn't mean it's not good. It's the best drink there is," I say, and he nods in agreement while filling his own cup with the same drink.

"One time when I was in college, I drank an entire twelve-pack in a day." We walk to an empty two-person table and settle into it.

"That's child's play. I've done twenty-four cans in a day," I say and sip the sugary liquid with a happy sigh. "I couldn't drink the stuff for a week, and I felt awful, but it was worth it."

Brad laughs. "I'm impressed. And how old were you when you did this?"

"Twelve. It *might* have been for a bet with my older brother. My mom was not happy, but I made twenty bucks." I laugh.

"You sound like you were a troublemaker. I can see it," Brad says with a smirk, leaning back in his chair.

"Listen, just because I have blue hair doesn't mean I'm trouble," I say with a self-conscious laugh. Usually, when guys insinuate that I'm some sort of 'trouble,' it has to do with my appearance. It's 2022, and yet people still have qualms about colorful hair. A frown creases Brad's face.

"What? I just meant you have that kind of personality. You're always saying cheeky things and teasing people. What does your hair color have to do with anything?" I blink at him, trying to come up with something that doesn't sound like an insecure teenager.

The thing is, I love having colorful hair. It's a way to make life less mundane and boring to me. Blue has stuck around for a while, but it's been purple and burgundy and a few other colors in the past. However, it's hard to be taken seriously with colorful hair in the corporate world. Also in the dating world, or at least with the guys I've dated.

So, over time, I've kept the hair but operated under the notion that most people find it immature at best.

"I tend to get judged a lot for the color, so I just assumed. I'm sorry." I bite my lip and swear I see his eyes flick to my mouth for a second.

"First of all, it's ridiculous for anyone to judge you based on your hair color. And second of all, your hair is beautiful, so I don't know why anyone would think anything other than that when they see you." A blush heats my face and Brad seems to realize what he said because he averts his gaze sheepishly.

A server saves the awkward silence that's fallen over us as he lists off our meal orders and sets them on the table. A small smile occupies my face for the rest of our lunch break, and not because the food here is delicious. But because Brad just called me beautiful—well, my hair at least—and he meant it. He was candid and sincere yet mature about everything.

Am I—could I be crushing on Brad Jennings?

CHAPTER 6

Brad Jennings

"I can't believe you're going to marry someone from the auditing team," I say to Callum. Zara and I are in his office reviewing some documentation to ensure nothing is missing before sending it over to Charlotte's team. Working with audit is a pain, one that plagues our whole team. Callum used to hate audit—and Charlotte, for that matter—with a passion. But now he's smitten with her.

"It's her only flaw," Callum says, making me chuckle. At least he still hates audit.

"Does drinking soda count as a flaw? Because she does that too," Zara chimes in, sharing a secret smile with me, reminding me of our lunch conversation. Lunch yesterday went better than expected. Even after I made things awkward by calling her beautiful so blatantly. She didn't seem put off by it, just a little shy. I'm hoping that means there's a chance for me with her.

"That's true," Callum sighs. "I've tried to tell her that all soda is essentially battery acid, but she doesn't listen."

"If drinking Dr Pepper is wrong, I don't want to be right," I say and Zara nods.

"Period." She holds a hand up for a high-five, and I hit her hand with a grin. I'm sure her word choice has something to do with TikTok, but the meaning is clear enough that I don't have to show my age by asking her. I guess there are plenty of people my age on TikTok, though; I'm just not one of them.

"I can't deal with you two," Callum grumbles.

"You love us." Zara laughs, but I can't because my brain is stuck on the last word in her sentence: *us*. I look over at her and take in her carefree smile. Her hair is down today, the shiny cobalt strands swishing against her back when she shifts in her chair. I'm sure it'll be up on top of her head by noon like it usually is when she's deep in coding. My fingertips twitch as I imagine what it would be like to run my hands through that hair.

Callum starts going over another line in the document, and I miss the transition back to work because I'm staring at Zara. When he asks me a question, I fumble for the answer, accidentally closing out the notes I had opened. Thankfully, I recover quickly and manage to give him the answer he was looking for.

The rest of the meeting is spent staring at my laptop screen and using all my resolve not to glance at Zara every time she speaks or moves. I only fail twice. Okay, three times, *sue me*. She looks extra pretty today with her hair down and her sweater sleeves tugged over her palms. What is it about a girl with oversized sleeves? It's too adorable, especially on someone like Zara.

"Okay, I'll let y'all get back to work. Thanks for being so cooperative. I know this isn't an enjoyable process," Callum says at the end of the meeting.

"You're welcome, boss," Zara replies cheekily while shutting her laptop.

"No problem," I tell him and shut my own. Zara walks out of the office, but Callum stops me from following.

"You alright, man? You've seemed a little off your game lately."

"Oh yeah, I'm fine! Just have a lot going on with this project," I say with a shrug. Callum is my best friend, but he's also my boss. I don't know what he would think about me pursuing Zara. It's not against any rules at Wreston, which is why he and Charlotte can be together, but it might be frowned upon with how closely Zara and I work together. I don't want to make a big deal out of something that hasn't even happened yet.

"Okay, well let me know if I put too much on your plate. I'm aware I expect a lot from you and Zara, but I know you're human, too."

I smile at his words. "I'll be sure to let you know," I say, and then walk out of his office before he can ask me anything else.

Zara is waiting outside of our cubicles, toying with the sleeves of her sweater. She looks up when I approach, a smile brightening her face.

"Hey! I was thinking of going to get hot cocoa from The Sweet Bean before getting back to work. Want me to grab you something?"

"That sounds great, but I could use some fresh air. I'll walk with you," I say, and her smile widens, making her eyes crinkle at the edges. Being the source of that smile makes warm satisfaction run through me.

"Even better!" She grabs her signature black messenger bag, and we walk side by side to the elevators. We manage to be the only ones on the elevator again, and silence settles over us for a moment. I tuck my hands into my hoodie pocket and rack my brain for the right topic of conversation.

"You're wearing jeans today," Zara blurts out, making me look over at her.

"Uh, yeah. It was pretty chilly this morning, so I figured it made more sense." She nods and I look back toward the elevator doors.

Zara speaks up again after a beat of silence. "They look nice." In my peripheral I see her toying with the sleeves of her sweater again. *Is she nervous?* The thought makes my stomach swoop.

"Thank you," I say right before the elevator doors slide open. The lobby is pretty calm today, so we don't have any bustling patrons to cover up our return to silence. I shouldn't have any problem talking to Zara, but I feel like I have to double and triple-check what I'm going to say for fear of pushing too much. Maybe that's why I haven't gotten anywhere with her, though. Maybe I need to be bold like I was at lunch.

Once we're outside on the sidewalk, I go to speak up. "Zara—"

"Watch out! Christmas cheer coming through!" a booming voice sounds out. Up ahead is an elf on a unicycle, barreling toward us at top speed. I snag Zara's arm and tug her out of the way of the rogue elf man.

She looks up at me with her body pressed against my chest and giggles. Her dark eyes sparkle under thick lashes coated in mascara. My breath is gone. I'm going to need resuscitation because Zara being this close has stolen all the oxygen from my lungs.

"Was that an elf on a unicycle?" She giggles again and it's infectious, making me chuckle with her.

"I think so." My voice is raspier than I intended, and Zara's giggles fade when our eyes lock once more. A stray blue lock of hair falls into her eyes, and I lift my hand to brush it away. Zara is frozen in my arms, watching me with her mesmerizingly dark eyes. Just as my fingers graze her hair, a truck horn blasts loudly.

Zara jumps back out of my arms. Whatever moment we were having is now gone. She tucks the strand I was reaching for behind her ear, not meeting my eyes.

I clear my throat. "We should probably get going; don't want to take too long." She nods in agreement, and we start toward The Sweet Bean.

There's no way I'm going to recover from her being in my arms. There was *something* between us, I'm sure of it. Something in her eyes. I glance down at her walking beside me and catch her watching me already. She snaps her head forward, but I grin because I know the truth.

She feels something more than friendship with me. And I'm going to make sure that feeling only grows. *Prepare to be wooed, Zara Thomas.*

CHAPTER 7

Zara Thomas

I click my pen over and over while staring blankly at my screen. Brad *held* me. He swept me into his arms, out of harm's way, like some superhero. And boy oh boy, did he have the muscles to match that superhero gesture. I bite my lip as I think of how secure I felt in his arms and how solid his chest was.

An email notification dings, shattering my daydream. I shake off the feeling. So what if Brad's strong arms felt amazing wrapped around me? That doesn't mean anything. Anyone would have gotten caught up in the moment. He was saving me from being run over by an elf, not trying to seduce me.

But his hand did reach up to brush away my hair ... *Nope.* Can't go there. I aggressively click my pen in an effort to expel the weird energy within me. There are so many reasons not to date Brad.

And yet, when I try to recall them, they seem impossible to grasp. Like sand through my fingertips. He's older than me, which is weird sometimes, but the gap isn't alarming by any means. He's my boss, kind of. Callum is my actual boss, but Brad is above me on the team hierarchy. That makes things complicated for sure. But is it complicated enough?

It would be if he were to reject me. Then I'd have to work with him daily while there's this awkward tension between us. But I can't seem to shake the feeling of him pulling me out of harm's way.

As my mind drifts back to that moment on the sidewalk, my hair starts to feel too hot on my neck. I stand up and flip my head upside down to twist it into a bun using the white scrunchie I keep on my wrist for this very purpose. When I raise my head, I can't help but look at Brad over the cubicle wall.

His eyes are trained on the screen as his fingertips glide across his keyboard. He tilts his head from side to side, stretching his neck. Since our coffee break, we've both been zoned in on work, so I'm sure his muscles are stiff. His clicking ceases and he stands up, lifting his arms in the air to stretch further. His hoodie lifts with the movement and my eyes widen.

There's not much to write home about lower back muscles. They're not a flashy muscle group like abs or biceps. But it's still abundantly clear that Brad works out. He just hides all of his work under hoodies and baggy shorts for some unfortunate reason. Suddenly, Brad twists his torso in my direction. I drop down to the ground, hitting my knees.

I press my lips together as pain shoots through my kneecaps and bang my fist softly on the rough office carpet. Not my smartest decision. Slowly, I push myself up, hoping not to attract Brad's attention.

I brush off my knees where crumbs and bits of paper have stuck to my sweatpants. I scrunch my nose at the sight. To think I was under the impression someone cleaned in here often. When I lift my head, I'm met with a devastating smirk.

"Everything okay, Zara?" The teasing lilt of Brad's voice lets me know I was caught. Heat flushes to my face as I nod.

I clear my throat. "Um–yeah!" I stumble over my words, trying for some kind of excuse. "A-actually, I was going to ask you for help on this project." I'm going to pretend that my subject shift was smooth and not absolutely atrocious.

Brad raises his eyebrows, that torturous smirk still playing on his lips. "Okay, let me see if I can help." He walks out of his cubicle, and I sink into my desk chair. If my back is to him, he can't see my blush and I can't see his lips. It's a win-win.

"So, what's going on?" Brad asks from behind me. I lift a slightly shaking hand and place it on my mouse. Then I move the cursor to point out the issue.

"Something is wrong with the coding for this button. I can't figure out what it is." This is true, but I'm sure if I spent more than a few minutes on it that I could figure it out on my own. I've never been one of those girls to feign ineptitude for attention, and bitterness twists in my stomach when this feels like that. How on earth did Charlotte manage to mix emotions with work? I develop a tiny crush and suddenly I'm floundering on the office carpet and asking for help on things I could likely handle on my own.

"May I?" He leans over me and gestures to where my hand is covering the mouse. I slide my fingers back and let them fall into my lap. Brad's chest presses into me softly, it barely qualifies as a touch, but it feels like flames across my back. I watch his large hand cover my mouse. It's almost comically small in his palm.

He's trapped me. My heart beats out of my chest when I feel his breath against the back of my head. His scent fills the space, a deep, musky fragrance with a tinge of sweetness. The kind of scent you burn on a cold night while cuddled up under a plaid blanket in a cabin somewhere.

"This line right here is your issue." Instead of using the cursor to show the code he's referencing, he lifts his opposite arm to point at the screen. I'm wrapped up in him, and yet we're barely touching. The urge to lean back against him hits me so hard that I get mental whiplash. I notice the problem with the line right away. I hate and love that I asked him to help me.

"I see," I breathe out. "Thank you." *What would it be like,* I wonder, *to lean back and just be held by him?*

"You're welcome," he says huskily. His arms leave their position around me, and he takes a step back. I reluctantly spin my chair around to face him, praying that my emotions aren't as noticeable as they feel.

He runs a hand through his hair, and I notice a slight tremor with the movement. Could he be as affected by me as I am by him? I cross my arms over my chest, hoping to still my frantic heart. I told myself not to get caught up in romanticism, and yet here I am, looking for signs. It doesn't make sense for someone like Brad to be interested in me. I'm far from what I imagine is his type.

"Let me know if you hit any other snags," Brad says, and I nod.

"Thanks again," I say quietly. He dips his chin, then leaves. I listen for the sound of him working again and hear him let out a deep sigh. The wall between our offices has never felt so thin.

CHAPTER 8

Brad Jennings

*S ilky blue hair sifts through my fingertips as deep
brown eyes gaze into my own. Her pale pink lips
part slightly, inviting me to tilt my head and lean in–*

I'm jolted awake at the sound of incessant vibrating near my ear. I groan and roll over to face my nightstand. My phone sits on a stand facing my bed, and Callum's name fills the screen. I scramble to sit up and yank my phone off the charger.

"Hello?" I answer, running a hand through my hair. *Is Charlotte okay? Is something wrong at Wreston? Is his mom hurt?* Every bad scenario barrages my mind all at one time.

"Brad, we have a tier 2 disaster protocol: the app isn't showing customers' savings accounts. Customers are flooding the system with complaints because they think their money is gone. I need you and Zara on this, now." Panic squeezes at my chest. This is my project; I can't have this go wrong. I could lose my job.

"Okay, I'll call Zara and get on my laptop right now." I slide out of bed and fumble in the dark to turn on my bedroom light.

"I can't risk this taking any longer than necessary. Call Zara and have her meet you at Wreston. The network is fast, and all of the database servers are there if you need them. I'll run interference with security and audit while you fix this issue."

I nod, then realize he can't see me. "Okay, I'm on it." The line goes dead after that, and I quickly yank on a pair of sweatpants and a hoodie, then shove my feet into socks and tennis shoes. After that, I press Zara's contact and tuck my phone in between my ear and shoulder so I can grab my laptop and keys.

The phone rings for what feels like an eternity. "Pick up, pick up, pick up," I mumble as the ringing continues.

Finally, she answers. "Hello?" Her voice is low and sleepy, almost stopping me in my tracks with how cute it sounds. *Get it together, Brad. You don't have time to think about how adorable she is.*

"Zara, I need you to meet me at Wreston. There's a problem with the app. Customers can't see their savings accounts." I pull open my apartment door as I speak, locking it behind me.

"*What?* Okay, I'll be there as soon as I can."

"See you there." She hangs up in a similar fashion to Callum. I'm only able to register what time it is once I get into my car. I scrub my hands over my face when I read *2 AM.*

My hands grip the freezing cold steering wheel as I drive. I blast the heat in an attempt to lessen the frigid temperatures. Two in the morning in November isn't exactly the most comfortable of climates. I rush to the office–possibly speeding, but there are no cops out to witness it–and arrive to a mostly empty parking lot. There's one car already here, and I'm assuming it belongs to the security guard because I know it's not Zara's.

I swipe my keycard to get into the building and the warm air inside thaws my skin, making me sigh in relief. After nodding to the security guard posted at the front desk, I press the button for the elevator. The lobby door slams open, making me jerk my head toward it.

Zara rushes in, her hair up in a wild-looking bun and her body covered in something that looks like a hoodie and a blanket had a baby. The elevator slides open, so I hold it for her.

"How bad is it?" she asks as soon as she steps onto the elevator. I step back and press the button for our floor.

"I don't know yet. Callum said to come straight here instead of working from home."

"So it's really bad." I glance over at her and catch her chewing her thumbnail.

"It's going to be okay. We'll find the problem, fix it, and then be out of here. Nothing to worry about." I try to soothe her with my words, but it doesn't seem to help. Her slightly puffy eyes are wide and worried.

"What if it's something I did? I could get fired. I haven't been here long. This could be the mistake that costs me my job–"

I cut her off, grabbing both of her hands. "Breathe, Z. It's going to be okay. No one is getting fired." *I hope.*

She blinks up at me.

"Did you just call me Z?" she asks quietly, tilting her head to the side. Her bun flops over with the movement, making me smile.

"Yeah, is that okay? Do you hate it?" She shakes her head, a small smile playing on her lips. The very lips I was dreaming about kissing not even thirty minutes ago.

"I like it." Her voice is as soft as her hands. I want to wrap this moment up and place it underneath the Christmas tree to have forever. When the elevator jerks to a stop, Zara jerks her hands back in surprise. Moment gone.

"Let's go fix this before the entire company has to wake up early," I say, and she nods. We speed over to our cubicle cluster. "Why don't you grab your laptop and set up at my desk? We'll need to do some pair programming to find what's gone wrong."

"Sounds good." She sets herself up on the right side of my desk, and I move my monitors around so she has room. Our quarters are still very close, but they need to be for this problem to be fixed.

We begin going through every line of code under the block related to the savings account portion of the app. It's tedious, but necessary. I can't afford to be unfocused, and yet Zara being so close to me makes it difficult to stay on task.

She smells like apple pie, which was never high on my list of favorite desserts, but she might change that. Our arms brush, and it sends sparks through me—the same as the very first time it happened. You'd think I'd be desensitized, considering how much we work together, but no. If anything, working so closely has made me hyperaware of every sensation Zara evokes within me.

I make myself study the code diligently, knowing both of our jobs are on the line, but in the back of my mind I'm constantly aware of how close she is and how absolutely gorgeous she is, even at 3 AM. After over an hour of work, Zara straightens in her chair next to me.

"Here!" She points at the screen. "The server team must have changed the DB server name when they performed the upgrade. The code is pointing to WBSVGDB1, and they set the new server up as WBSVGDB01."

I confirm her finding, and we get to work making the change to the new server name. We run some unit tests and push the changes into production. After a call to Callum, we confirm that the app is up and running properly again.

We slump back into our chairs once we're done, the adrenaline of the situation now gone. Our shoulders brush, the movement making me glance over at her. Her eyes are half-open. I'd give anything to be the one who sees her like this out of the office. The one who gets to brush away the stray hairs escaping her bun and hold her close as she falls asleep.

"I guess we need to get started on documentation," Zara says with a yawn. I turn back toward the screens so she doesn't think I'm staring too much.

"Yeah, let's get this finished so we can get home and maybe get a little more sleep before work starts."

Zara sighs. "I won't be able to get back to sleep, even as tired as I am. Once I'm up, I'm up for good." I shoot her a sympathetic smile.

"Well, then maybe we can grab some coffee at The Sweet Bean. They should be open by the time we finish up here."

"You don't want to try and get some sleep?"

"I'll be fine," I say and wave her off with a smile. The truth is, if it was just me, I'd go home and sleep until right before I had to come back here. But I'd choose more time with Zara–especially an adorably sleepy Zara–than rest any day.

CHAPTER 9

Zara Thomas

W hy is it so wonderfully warm in this office today? Usually, the temperature is too cold or too hot to be comfortable, but not today. Today, when I need to stay awake, it's the perfect temperature to make me want to doze off at my desk.

It's almost lunch time, and my body is finally getting hit with the exhaustion that this morning's emergency caused. I can't count the times I've almost faceplanted into my keyboard while propping myself up using my elbow.

My phone buzzes, making me jump out of my almost-nap yet again. An incoming call from my mom. I pick it up and press *answer* with a frown. My mom never calls while I'm at work. She's always been a rule-follower and makes sure she doesn't cross any boundaries. It must be important.

"Hey, Mom," I greet her, trying to lace my tired voice with some sort of cheer so she doesn't worry about me.

"Hi sweetpea," she says back, and I smile at the sound of my childhood nickname. I live five hours away from my family, so I don't get to see them often. This makes every reminder of their love all the more special.

"Everything okay? You don't usually call while I'm working."

"Oh—yes, well I thought you'd be on your lunch break," she stammers, and a weight settles in my stomach. Something is wrong. My mom knows my work schedule to a tee. There's no way she thought I was on my lunch break early.

"I'm not yet, no. What's wrong?"

"I wish I could tell you in person, but I don't want to wait until the holidays. Those might be changing, anyway..." she trails off, making worry rise like bile in my throat.

"What is it, Mom?" I can't keep the panic out of my voice.

She lets out a heavy sigh. "Your father and I have decided to separate." I suck in a breath. I've always admired my parents' marriage. They never fought, always spent time together, and talked about how much they loved each other constantly. Everything seemed perfect.

"What? Why? You guys love each other." The pause on the other end of the phone is haunting.

"We just need some time to sort things out. We've been growing apart for quite some time now, but it's become more apparent as of late." I want to scream at her formal tone. She's making it sound like a business decision and not the end of her marriage to my own father.

"So what does this mean? You're still married, right?"

"Your father has moved in with your uncle Loid for now so that I can have some space. I will update you on holiday arrangements within the week."

"Okay," I say, unable to come up with anything more. My parents are separated. They might get divorced. I'd always assumed they'd be together until death, like their vows said.

"I have to go now, a client of mine is calling. I love you."

"I love you, too." My phone clatters against my desk. When I was about twelve, a lot of my friends' parents got divorced. I watched their lives change dramatically over the course of that year while mine remained normal. A few of them even stayed at my house as a refuge during that time. And now, at twenty-two years old, I'm going through what they did. I feel like Jennifer Garner in *13 Going on 30*, except I've gone to the past instead of the future.

My emotional state is weak from the exhaustion and stress of this morning, so I'm not surprised when tears begin to burn the back of my eyes. I hold my face in my hands and hunch over in my chair. I don't even have the energy to worry if anyone sees me when I begin to cry and sniffle.

"Zara?" I hear Brad's voice nearby, but I ignore it. I don't want to talk to anyone while I'm like this. I debate making a mad run for the women's bathroom so I can cry without anyone noticing, but before I can make up my mind, my office chair spins around slowly, and warm hands grasp my wrists. "Z, what's wrong?" Light fills my vision when gentle but strong hands tug my stiff fingers away from my face. "Talk to me, sweetheart." His term of endearment surprises me, but my mind is swimming in thoughts about my parents, so I don't have time to think on it.

I shake my head, squeezing my eyes shut. Brad releases my wrists and I wipe at my eyes to clear them. After blinking a few times, his face comes into focus. He's down on his knees in front of my chair, concern lining his face.

"I-it's nothing. I'm fine," I rasp out, but he shakes his head, not believing me.

"It's not nothing. You can talk to me." He pushes back my hair, tucking it behind my ear, making my breath catch. I meet his gaze. The sincerity within his eyes makes me voice my thoughts.

"My parents just decided to separate; they might be getting a divorce." My voice trembles. "Ugh, I'm getting worked up over something so many people go through as kids. I'm an adult, I should be more mature." I swipe away the remainder of my tears with a huff.

"It's okay to be hurt by this. You're not immature. I'd be upset if my parents separated, and I'm older than you." I see him cringe at the end of his sentence, and I wonder why. I've thought about our nine-year age gap, but I don't think it's too drastic.

I sigh. "It's just so unexpected. They've been happy my whole life. I used to want a relationship like theirs, and now it feels like a lie."

"I'm sorry." Those two words held so much emotion they took me by surprise. That phrase—I'm sorry—can either sound shallow or deep, and his sincerity went deeper than an ocean. "Is there anything I can do to help?" I look at him on his knees in front of me, and warmth floods my chest. He really cares for me.

"Being able to talk about it has helped already. I'm not sure there's much else you can do."

"How about lunch?" he asks, pushing himself to his feet, his six foot frame now towering over me. "We can go just us or invite Charlotte and Callum."

My smile is small but sincere. "I think lunch sounds great. It can be just us." A blush heats my face when he grins. I scramble to clarify. "Just because I don't want to tell anyone else yet."

He nods in understanding.

"Whatever you need, Z. I'm your man." He pulls me to my feet, and my heart skips.

My man, I muse. Interesting choice of words. As he leads me toward the elevators, hand on my lower back, I find I don't hate the sound of his phrase.

CHAPTER 10

Zara Thomas

"**A**nd just what did he mean by *sweetheart*, Calypso?" I look down at my canine confidant. She tilts her head to the right, her black ears flopping with the movement. Sighing, I pet her. "Yes, it is confusing."

I've spent the morning mulling over the shifts in Brad's behavior toward me. It's hard not to when he was so tender—and *romantic*—this week. After coming out of the haze of realizing my family is changing in a monumental way, my brain chose to latch onto the fact that Brad has been acting like much more than a coworker. A train of thought that is currently torturing me. And since I don't want to talk to anyone about it, my dear black lab, Calypso, has become my listening ear.

I pull a brush through my freshly dried hair. Today I'll be heading to the spa for Charlotte's bachelorette party. I'm looking forward to the pampering, for sure, but also the opportunity for girl talk. Maybe I can fish for advice without giving away who I'm talking about. Charlotte is like a bloodhound when it comes to relationship gossip though, so I might have to hold back and just try to enjoy the relaxing time. I'd probably be a whole lot more successful at chilling today if I didn't know that I'd have to see Brad at the dance hall later tonight when we meet up with the guys.

What if he asks me to dance? I groan at the thought and study my reflection in the mirror. My fair skin is rosy just thinking of Brad asking me. I'm doomed. I've already succumbed to fanciful ideas and ridiculous notions. He called me sweetheart, so what? Maybe he does that all the time with others. We do live in the south. Just because I've never heard him say it to any other woman doesn't mean he hasn't.

I'm about to voice my woes to Calypso again when my phone starts buzzing on my bathroom counter. My brother Drake's name appears on my screen.

"Hello?" I answer it and walk out of the bathroom, still running a brush through my hair.

"Hey, where are you?" Drake asks. I plop down onto my brown leather couch.

"My apartment, why?" I smile as Calypso snuggles into her fluffy dog bed across the room.

"Are you sitting down?" I don't miss the tinge of worry in his voice. I set my brush down beside me and tuck my legs under me.

"Yes, actually. What's going on?"

He sighs. "Mom and Dad are selling the house." My heart drops to my stomach. I knew my mom said there would be changes, but I didn't think this would be one of them.

"What? Why?"

"Dad is moving into some apartment in Charlotte." He pauses, letting that sink in. My family has lived in Charleston my whole life. I moved here for school, and they all acted like I was leaving the country. Now Dad is just up and leaving? "Mom says the house is too big for her. She didn't tell me until this morning. Someone already put a bid in. They're closing right after Thanksgiving."

I fall back against the couch. My childhood home ... *gone*. Flashes of memories of opening Christmas presents, blowing out birthday candles, and playing hide and seek all pass through my mind. Tears burn the back of my eyes.

"I didn't realize it was all so serious. She said they were just separated. I thought maybe they would work things out." My voice cracks, and I hate it. I don't want to cry again.

"I'm sorry, Zara. I don't think that's going to happen. I think this has been a long time coming for them, but it feels fast to us."

"Because they didn't say anything!" A bolt of anger strikes me, and I stand up. "We could have helped them. Stopped this."

"I love you, Zara, you know that. And I hate this as much as you do. But I don't think us knowing earlier would have stopped this from happening. You know how Mom is when she gets an idea in her head." He sighs. "And Dad has basically run away from the whole family. There's nothing we can do now but deal with it all."

I push a hand through my hair and frown. I wish that wasn't true. "I love you too, Drake. I guess you're right, I just wish there was a way we could keep the house."

"If Annabeth and I didn't just buy our house, we'd try to buy it. But we couldn't swing it so fast."

I sigh at his words, resigned. I can't afford that large of a home, and I work five hours away in Atlanta. "Will we even have Thanksgiving at their house this year?"

"We'll host it at our house. Mom wants to be moved out quickly, so I guess she'll want us to help."

I don't even get a chance to have one last holiday in the house.

"Okay, I'll try to take off an extra day or two and stay long enough to help." The weight of what is happening begins to settle like a cement brick on my chest.

"That would be good. I'll see you then. Call me if you need me," he says, brotherly concern coating his voice. The sound of it only makes my tears come faster.

"I will," I whisper, then we hang up. I drop my phone on the couch and then sink to the floor.

Calypso pads over to me, nudging her nose against my knee. I wrap an arm around her and hug her furry body close. My heart aches and my eyes burn, and I wish I had someone here to comfort me. My mind brings up the image of Brad on his knees in my tiny cubicle, concern lining his face as he held my hands. But he's not here, and he's not mine, so it's foolish to think of that now.

I shake off the thought and hold Calypso a little tighter. I have no idea how I'm going to face my parents' divorce, losing my childhood home, and letting go of all of our holiday traditions all at once. This is going to be the worst holiday season yet.

CHAPTER 11

Brad Jennings

T he girls climb into the limo, and I anxiously wait for Zara to appear. After comforting her earlier this week, I've been on edge about being around her tonight. I don't regret what I said, but I'm nervous that the attention wasn't as welcome as I originally thought.

I can't help but frown when the limo door shuts and Zara is nowhere in sight. I want to ask about her, but after slipping up and telling the guys I liked someone while we were playing poker earlier, I don't want them to get suspicious.

"Where's Zara?" Callum asks, drawing me into his conversation with Charlotte.

"She texted that she couldn't make it to the spa. Hopefully she meets us at the dance hall!" Worry settles in my stomach, and I pull out my phone to text her. We haven't really texted each other much though, which causes me to pause. I could be overdoing it. *If she doesn't show up at the dance hall, I'll text,* I decide. Then I'll just be seen as a worried friend and not as the guy who's falling for her and is bad at hiding it.

The ride to the dance hall feels agonizingly long as I continue worrying about Zara. She was so broken up about her parents' separation. She's usually upbeat and relaxed around the office. I've never seen her so upset before. I run a hand through my hair and sigh. My brother JJ glances at me, curiosity shining in his eyes, so I look over at Callum and feign interest in what he's talking about. As per usual, when it comes to Zara, I'm a mess. It's a miracle I've been able to conceal my feelings this long.

"Let's go! I don't want to sit on the sidelines all night." Charlotte drags Callum toward the dance floor when a new song starts. "See you out there!" she yells back at us.

We haven't been here long, but I knew Charlotte wouldn't waste any time tonight. Ever since we started working on the app project together,

I've heard about her love of dancing. Callum isn't much for crowds or dancing, but I know he'd do anything for her.

I'm scanning the crowd when my eyes catch on cobalt blue hair. My heart skips in my chest.

"Zara!" I push up out of my chair as fast as possible. She stops at the table and immediately I know she's not okay. Her eyes are rimmed in black and her smile is weak.

"Sorry I'm late, I had a family thing today," she says to all of us at the table.

"Are you okay? We missed you at the spa," Grace speaks up and the other girls nod in agreement.

"I'm alright! Ready to party." Zara tries for a big smile, but it's easy to see she'd rather be anywhere else.

"Have you eaten?" I ask her, not caring if the other guys catch on at this point. My only thoughts are about taking care of her. She shakes her head no. "Come on," I say with a soft smile and gesture for her to follow me.

I direct her toward the food counter in silence. The last thing I want is for her to feel like I'm only walking with her to pry information out of her. Once we're in line I feel her eyes on me, so I look down at her. Vulnerability shows in her gorgeous brown eyes, making my heart ache.

"Do you want to talk about it?" I ask. She shrugs, tearing her gaze from me. She keeps her eyes on the ground as we move forward in the line. "You don't have to. We can just..." I pause, searching for the right word. "Be." A ghost of a smile lifts her pink lips, and she nods.

It's our turn at the counter and Zara orders a cheeseburger and Dr Pepper. I catch her smiling even more when she says the drink and warmth floods my chest. Even if we are just friends, making her smile like that means so much to me. I gently move her aside when she pulls out her debit card and place my own order–the exact same as hers.

"Brad, I can pay–" I cut her off with a wave of my hand and quickly swipe my card. The cashier gives me a knowing look. Surely if I'm this obvious to a stranger then I must be to Zara as well, but if I am she makes no indication of knowing. She just thanks me quietly and stands by the pickup counter.

Our food is ready quickly, and I grab the bag while Zara holds our drinks. I wonder if anyone saw us if they'd think we're dating. I shake off the errant thought and focus on making sure Zara is taken care of.

"Let's see if we can find someplace quieter," I say over the music, and she nods. We weave through the crowd, and I spot an open corner table far away from the stage and speakers.

She slides into a chair, and I sit in one on the opposite side of her. The music is thankfully softer over here and the atmosphere feels much more private and quaint even though there are plenty of people around us.

"Thank you for this. The food and the table and, well, everything," Zara says as she pulls out a foil-wrapped burger.

"Of course. I wanted to be sure you were okay," I tell her sincerely.

"I wish I could say I was, but I'd be lying." She sighs. "I spent most of the morning crying on the floor of my apartment." She cringes and meets my eyes. "That might be oversharing. Sorry."

I shake my head. "Z, you can tell me anything. I won't judge you." Her smile undoes me. Each one she gives me feels like completing a coding project on the first try. They feel that hard to earn tonight.

"If you say so." She breathes out a laugh. "My brother called and told me not only are my parents separated, but they're getting a divorce and my mom is selling my childhood home." She pauses to take a bite of her burger.

"I'm sorry, that's awful. Can you convince her to keep the house?"

She shakes her head as she finishes chewing. "Nope, apparently she put it on the market without telling anyone. Now she's wanting to move out during Thanksgiving, and I'm supposed to come help. I don't even get to have Thanksgiving or Christmas there one last time." She lets out a frustrated huff. "I probably sound like I'm whining, I'm sorry."

"Don't be sorry. I meant what I said earlier about no judgment. I'd be frustrated too if I were you. So, you're going to help her move out?" I ask, hoping she'll continue talking and not feel like I don't care. I'd listen to her for hours if it made her feel better.

"Yes," she groans. "I don't want to deal with any of it. My brother lives up in Charleston with his wife, so he doesn't have to travel, and he has someone to help him through it. Meanwhile I have to drive five hours by myself and face it all alone. I just know my mother is going to drive me crazy too." She pinches the bridge of her nose with her eyes shut. "I'm getting a headache just thinking about it."

An idea comes to me that is absolutely ridiculous. So ridiculous that I shouldn't say it at all. *And yet...*

"I could come with you," I blurt out and Zara's eyes snap open. I jump to explain. "I could drive so you don't have to, and then be a buffer while we're there so you don't have to deal with the drama."

"It's Thanksgiving, I couldn't ask you to miss out on time with your family." Hope rises in my chest. *She's not saying no...*

"It would save me a lot of trouble, actually. My parents like to spend the holidays badgering me about why I'm not married yet. It's only going to be worse this year because JJ and Hallie are newly-weds."

She purses her lips, thinking. "It's too much to ask of you."

"It's not. I've never been to Charleston, either. So that's another plus." I take a bite of my burger and try to look like I'm not hanging on her every word.

"If you're sure it's not too much of an inconvenience, then I think I'll take you up on it. It's going to be miserable, though. My mom is going to say outrageous things, and there's going to be heavy stuff you'll get roped into moving because you look strong, and–"

"You think I look strong?" I ask with a smirk. She dips her head, a smile playing on her lips.

"Are you fishing for compliments, Bradley?" Her use of my full name flips a switch inside of me. And that switch is apparently connected to wanting to kiss her because now that's all I can think about.

"Just clarifying," I say, my voice coming out in a rasp.

She giggles. "Don't make me regret signing up to spend five hours in a car with you."

"You can't back out now, Z." I grin at her while a plan forms in my mind.

I'm going to make sure Zara has the best trip possible and, in the process, show her exactly how much she means to me.

CHAPTER 12

Brad Jennings

Okay, I can do this. Inhaling deeply, I push open my car door and get out. I pull my phone out of my pocket and check for Zara's unit number. After confirming for the fifth time this morning that her apartment is in fact #352, I look through my back window to make sure none of the road trip essentials I'd brought got jostled about during my drive here.

My blue cooler filled with cold Dr Pepper–plus a few water bottles for the illusion of health–sits secure in the floorboard, and the bag of snacks in the seat above it looks fine. The extra blanket and pillow I brought seem like a bit much now, but I figured she might want them if she doesn't bring her own. I tap the top of the car and nod. This will ensure we have a good start to the trip.

Bushes with browning leaves line the walkway. The wind rustles them as I walk up to the door, and the chill cuts through my jacket. I use the reflection of the glass doors to study my clothing. This morning I chose jeans, a flannel shirt, and a puffer jacket. Did I base my outfit today on Zara's minimal commentary on my looks? Yes, yes, I did. I'm not ashamed of it either.

Warm air with the subtle scent of Pine Sol hits me whenever I open the door to her building. A lanky, bored-looking security guard sits at a round desk in the middle of the lobby. He doesn't even look up when I come in. I frown as I press the 'up' button on the elevator. He's not keeping anyone safe. An unreasonable instinct to protect Zara sparks to life inside of me. Maybe I'll suggest moving to a safer building on our drive.

I step on the elevator and ride to the third floor while tapping my fingers against the side of my leg. I'm determined to make this trip great for Zara, but I'm still nervous about being on the road for so long alone with her. It will definitely test if we should date or not. Road trips tell you a lot about a person. Do they chew loudly? Do they sing in the car? Are they good with directions? So many questions to be answered and assessments to be made. Though I doubt anything Zara could do would make me think less of her.

I step out of the elevator and walk down the dimly lit hallway. A few of the fluorescents are out above, and one is flickering at the end of the hall. The wallpaper is yellowing and peeling at the corners. It's not a pleasant sight and furthers my desire for Zara to be somewhere else. I find Zara's door and knock before I have to spend any longer in the dingy hallway.

The door flies open and Zara blinds me with a stunning smile before spinning around and rushing back inside. "Come on in! I have to throw a few things into my backpack then I'll be ready," she says over her shoulder. I step into the small apartment, the scent of sugar cookies in the air. A black dog comes around the corner and pads over to me.

I place my hand above the dog's nose, and I'm rewarded with an investigative sniff before it leaves in the direction Zara went. Closing the door behind me, I walk further inside. A wooden wick candle crackles atop an acrylic coffee table, likely the source of the sweet vanilla scent. The entire apartment feels warm and cozy yet very modern. There's abstract art on the walls that are mostly swipes of earth tones and gold shimmer, and blankets are tossed over the worn leather couch. Somehow, it's both unexpected and yet perfect for Zara.

"Sorry about that, I couldn't find my purse Chapstick and I realized that my purse Chapstick was actually my bathroom Chapstick because I ran out of the original purse Chapstick. And then I went to get my nightstand Chapstick but that is now my desk Chapstick." She lifts her hands in the air with a huff. I blink at her, and she starts to laugh.

"I didn't know someone could have so many Chapsticks," I say, and she laughs some more.

"Soft lips are important to me," she says with a smile that is–dare I say it–*flirty*. Then she leans over and purses said lips to blow out the nearby candle.

"Noted," I rasp out, unable to come up with anything else. She slings a black and white checkered backpack over her shoulder before pursing her lips and whistling softly. The black dog from earlier bounces out of a nearby room and over to her side.

"Aunt Kelsey will be here soon," she coos while petting the calm dog. "And I'll be back in a couple of days. Stay out of trouble." She scratches under the dog's chin with an adoring smile on her face.

"What's their name?" I ask.

"Her name is Calypso," she says with another showstopping smile. "She keeps me company in this little matchbox of an apartment." I don't comment on the size of her apartment, but it is quite small. It's not as small as a studio, but it's not much bigger than that either. "I have a sitter that comes and watches her while I'm out of town. She'll be here in an hour, but Calypso can hang out until then, so we don't have to wait."

"Okay, great. Do you need any help with your bags?" I ask her and glance down at her large, gray suitcase propped up against the wall.

"I can get it! It has wheels." She yanks the elephant-seal-sized suitcase off the wall and grunts as she tugs it behind her. Her backpack slides down her shoulder into the crook of her arm, forcing her to stop to pull it back up.

"Z, let me take it," I say and reach for the handle. My thumb covers her pinky and her breath catches. Zara's chocolate irises gaze up at me, meeting my own before flickering down to my lips. *Does she want to kiss me?*

Suddenly, the warmth of her hand disappears and the full weight of the cold plastic handle falls into my hands, making me almost drop it. She steps away, repositioning her backpack on her shoulder while avoiding my eyes.

"We should get going, it's a long drive," she says quietly, and I sigh. *Way to make the start of our trip awkward, Brad.* Now instead of starting off strong, I'm going to spend the first part of the trip recovering. And hopefully, we don't spend the next five hours in awkward silence.

CHAPTER 13

Zara Thomas

B rad is kind of hot. Okay, not kind of, he *is* hot. He's got this whole casual lumberjack vibe today with his flannel. It's unexpected and disconcerting, which is probably why I almost kissed him like an idiot in my apartment. I could have made our trip incredibly awkward if I did that and he didn't want me to.

Though, judging by our current uncomfortable silence, not kissing him hasn't saved us from that fate. I bite my lip and glance over at him. His fingers tap out a soundless beat on the steering wheel as he keeps his eyes on the road. If he senses me staring, he doesn't show it.

Suddenly, he clears his throat, making me jump. "There's drinks and snacks in the back seat, by the way," he says, and I nod even though he's not looking at me.

"You didn't have to do that," I say with a smile. It's hard to believe he offered to drive and help move, and the fact that he also brought road trip snacks speaks volumes to the kind of man he is.

"It was selfish, really," he says with a grin. "I didn't want to go five hours without snacks and caffeine."

"Still, I appreciate it."

Silence consumes the car once more. I fiddle with the hem of my black hoodie, then adjust in my seat. I'm tempted to reach for my phone, but it feels rude to do that so early into the drive.

"Twenty questions!" I blurt out, startling Brad. I mentally face-palm at my lack of a transition. I must seem so eloquent. "Let's play twenty questions to pass the time," I elaborate and Brad smiles.

"Sounds like a great idea." I see him relax into his seat more and wonder if he was nervous as well.

"I'll go first. What's your favorite season?"

"Definitely winter." His tone is matter-of-fact. A blur of brown, barren trees surrounds us. Though most would deem the sight as sad, I love trees in winter. The only thing I'd love more is if they were heavy with snow. But we'd have to be heading further north for that.

"Mine too!" I smile at him.

"It's too hot in the south to like spring or summer," he says.

"Plus, winter is the coziest season." I glance at him and imagine what it would be like to cozy up with him in particular. Why is it becoming easier and easier to picture?

"That's true. Well, speaking of coziness, what's your favorite way to relax at the end of the day?"

"I like to get into my pajamas, make a cup of hot cocoa and watch *Catfish*," I say, and he laughs.

"You watch reality shows?" I raise my eyebrows at his tone.

"What's wrong with that?" So much is wrong with it, actually. I'm pretty sure it rots my brain a little more each time I watch it, but it's something I can put on and not have to think about anything. And watching it may or may not make me feel better about my love life...or lack thereof.

"They don't call it trash tv for nothing," he jokes, and I gasp in faux shock.

"It's quality entertainment, I'll have you know!" I hit his arm lightly and he laughs some more. The sound fills the car and makes me giggle with him. I feel lighter than I have since finding out about my parents' separation. Even hanging out with my friends hasn't made me feel this way.

"I'll take your word for it," he says once his laughter subsides.

"How can you judge it without watching it?" I ask, keeping my tone playful.

"That's fair. I guess I'll reserve judgment just so I don't have to watch it." My head hits the seat rest when I throw it back, laughing.

"Fine then, since my show is *trash*, what do you watch?" I ask him, my curiosity peaking when he shifts in his seat as if he's uncomfortable.

"Baseball, mostly," he says, making me narrow my eyes.

"You're lying."

He gapes. "I am not! You can ask Callum and JJ, we watch baseball together all the time."

"I believe that, but it's not what you watch when you're alone." He presses his lips together in response. "Tell me!" I say while shifting in my seat to look at him more directly.

"Kidsbakingchampionship," he mumbles the string of words so low I almost don't catch it.

"*Kids Baking Championship.* That's what you watch?" I ask with a giggle. His cheeks tint a rosy red.

"I like rooting for the kids, okay? And I love dessert," he defends himself.

"I think it's sweet." He shakes his head at my words. "It is! It's cute," I say and immediately want to sew my mouth shut. His eyebrows raise slightly, but his mouth tips up in a smile that shows me he doesn't think I'm weird for saying what I did.

"If you say so." My face warms as I consider that he might like my accidental flirtations from today.

I feel like the tiny part of me that hopes Brad likes me is growing bigger and bigger. It's taking over the rational parts of my brain and making me slip up and say things that I might come to regret. But I need to be strong during this trip. Crossing a line with Brad is too risky when I don't know for sure how he feels. The consequences are too great.

But when we slip back into conversation, I can't help but notice just how comfortable it is. And how I've never felt this way with anyone else before.

This trip is going to be dangerous ...

CHAPTER 14

Brad Jennings

I can't remember the last time I laughed this much. My sides are aching, and my face feels sore from smiling so much. I've liked Zara since she started working with us, but our time alone has only solidified my feelings. Every time I glance over at her it's like completing another side of a Rubik's cube. Her smile makes everything fall into place.

"I'm going to grab a Dr Pepper, do you want one?" she asks during a break in our conversation.

"That'd be great, thanks," I say with a smile. She reaches into the backseat, her body leaning closer to mine. Her scent washes over me and I'm reminded of holding her close on the sidewalk. My mind toys with the image, changing the ending of that moment to one where I have the courage to kiss her. The image shatters, however, when Zara pulls herself back to the front, slightly hitting my arm with one of the cold bottles.

"Sorry!" she says.

I shake my head, both to reassure her and to throw the rogue thought away.

"No worries," I say, keeping my eyes on the road. Up ahead a dark cloud looms. I checked the weather before we left, but there wasn't anything to worry about. There was a hurricane coming into Florida, but it was forecasted to stay further south and not hit us.

"That cloud looks a little ominous," Zara comments and I nod.

"Can you check the weather? I thought we were supposed to have clear skies all the way there." Out of the corner of my eye I see her pick up her phone.

"I don't have any signal." She sighs. "Surely it won't be too bad though."

As we continue on the road, the sky darkens more and more until it seems as if it's nighttime. Then the rain comes. Cars ahead are riding their brakes; some even have their hazards on. I can't be frustrated though, because the rain is coming in heavy sheets.

I squint through the darkness and focus on the red taillights ahead. Strong winds blow the car to the side, forcing me to constantly pull the car back into the center of the lane. It's getting harder and harder to make out what's ahead.

"It's pretty bad," I yell over the roaring rain.

"I can't see a thing," Zara yells back, and I hear the concern in her voice. I wish I could reach over to comfort her, but this is a two-hands-on-the-steering-wheel kind of moment.

We hit a puddle of water and hydroplane a little, sending my heart into overdrive. I can feel Zara's panic coming off her in waves. I put on my right blinker.

"I'm going to pull off the road and wait this out. I don't think it's safe to keep going." I think I hear her sigh in relief, but it's hard to know for sure with the storm raging. I get us off the road safely and put the car in park. After taking off my seatbelt, I glance at Zara.

She's looking out the passenger window, her bottom lip tucked in her teeth.

"Z," I say. She turns her head to look at me. "Are you okay?" Her brown eyes are wide, but she nods slowly.

"I'm okay. I hate driving in the rain, and riding passenger wasn't much better." I nod in understanding then grab my phone from the cubby below the dash. No signal.

I sigh. "No way of knowing how long this thing is going to last. I guess we're stuck here for a little while." I shift to face her in my seat. "There's a blanket in the back if you want to try to take a nap until it's over," I offer, and Zara leans her seat back then turns onto her side to face me. This feels...intimate. My heart skips when her eyes meet mine.

"I might do that. Can't be anxious if you're asleep, right?" She huffs out a nervous laugh and I frown. After grabbing the blanket from behind us, she drapes it over herself. An odd sensation falls over me seeing her under my blanket. I've used it many times on my own couch and bed. It feels like something a girlfriend would borrow, not a coworker.

"You're safe, Z, I'll make sure of it," I say, and she gives me a brief smile before closing her eyes. I watch her, noting the downward tilt of her mouth and the slight furrowing of her brows. Even with her eyes closed I can tell she's worried.

Lightning flashes across the sky and a roar of thunder follows, shaking the car. Zara jumps and instinctively I reach out to her. I grab her hand and hold it tight.

"You're okay," I say, keeping my eyes on hers. She nods and relaxes into the seat as I rub my thumb over the back of her hand.

"I'm sorry," she says, her voice almost blending in with the rain. "I was in an accident when I was in high school. It was raining one night, and we hydroplaned and slid off the road. Nobody got hurt, but it was pretty scary, and I haven't gotten over it."

I squeeze her hand. "I'm sorry that happened to you." She gives me a weak smile and squeezes my hand back. The gesture sends a jolt through me. *She's not pulling away.*

"Thank you for talking me through it."

"I'll always be here for you, Zara," I say while holding her gaze. Their usual deep chocolate color darkens in the dim light, resembling a night sky. They crinkle at the edges as she smiles, and I know I'm in trouble.

I'm falling in love with Zara Thomas, and she doesn't even know I like her.

CHAPTER 15

Zara Thomas

Brad held my hand until the storm passed, and I didn't hate the feeling. No, I loved it. His touch was comforting and steady. Eventually, I managed to fall asleep, and I woke up still holding his hand. I know his arm must have been killing him reaching awkwardly across the console, but he didn't complain.

Even now, he's smiling contentedly as we close in on Charleston. My mind has been spiraling since I woke up. I can't stop reliving all of the moments we've had together over the past month and even before that. There have been so many moments that seemed romantic to me, but maybe they weren't to him. Maybe this is his version of friendship. Friends can hold hands in a storm, I guess.

I look at him as we pull off the road into a gas station parking lot. What if I just asked him? We're both adults. Surely we could handle one awkward moment. Maybe it wouldn't ruin my career to ask where we stand. My stomach clenches at the thought. I don't think I could get fired, but it could make our working relationship awkward enough to make one of us have to leave.

"I'm going to get gas before we get into Charleston so we don't have to worry about it," he explains. I watch him through the window as he pays then starts pumping gas. He didn't even ask about me paying for or at least splitting the gas bill to get here. Surely it costs a lot to drive five hours, not to mention the amount of time on the side of the road with the car running. That seems like a boyfriend thing to do, too.

Even if he is doing this in a romantic way, I feel far from ready for a relationship. The relationship I've idolized for so long has just crumbled before my eyes. I'm currently on my way to sweep up the rubble. And yet ... I feel like I have to know.

After a short while, he's back in the car and looking at me with that easygoing smile that's been making my heart flutter more and more. He tilts his head to the side in question.

"You okay? Do you need anything?"

Before I can overthink any longer, I just go for it. "Why did you hold my hand for so long?" I keep going, though my heart is trying to jump out of my chest. "And why did you come all this way for me? And call me *sweetheart* the other day?" The questions come out in rapid succession, and with each one, regret settles over me like a wet blanket. He blinks at me in surprise and my stomach sinks.

His hand reaches up and rakes through his hair, mussing it slightly as he sighs. I glance at my door handle and wonder how fast I can get the door open if I throw up right now. Because I feel like I just might.

"I've had a–" he cuts himself off, making a face and shaking his head. "A crush sounds so childish, but I don't know another word for it." My mouth drops open slightly. "I've liked you for a long time, Zara," he begins again, looking at me, nervousness written all over his face. "I've been afraid of telling you, and now certainly isn't the best timing considering where we're heading, but it's true. I can't get you out of my head. Everything about you drives me crazy in the best way and–well, I've spent the past month falling for you. There. I said it." He takes a deep breath then lets it out.

I fall back against my seat and stare straight ahead out the windshield. I've spent the past month telling myself not to think Brad was interested in me, and here he is, telling me he's been pining after me without me knowing. My ridiculous romantic heart was right for once.

Half of me is celebrating, popping champagne like Michael in *The Office*. While the other half is in full-on panic mode. I thought he'd tell me he liked me as a friend or–at most– liked me enough to go on a date. Not that he's been falling for me. I didn't expect this at all, and my mind is reeling as a result.

"Z?" Brad's quiet voice cuts through my mental tailspin.

"I-I'm sorry, this is just a lot to process. And between the storm and the drama with my parents, I feel a little emotionally fragile." I chance a look at him. Instead of anger or frustration, I find understanding and compassion.

"Don't be sorry. I was trying to hold back, but I couldn't lie to you when you asked. I'll be here for you as a friend during this trip, like I told you before we came. And whenever you want to talk about being more than that or staying the same, I'll be here." His smile is reassuring and warms my heart.

"Thank you," I say, and realize just how much I've said that to him recently. He's done so many kind things for me. I'm going to have a lot to think about when it comes to him, that's for sure.

CHAPTER 16

Brad Jennings

Confessing that you're falling in love with a woman makes for an awkward remaining drive. It worked out in my favor, though, that Zara asked with only thirty minutes left in the trip. Also, being in Charleston meant Zara could tell me about where she grew up instead of descending into torturous silence.

Pastel-colored houses shining from fresh rain line the road as we near Zara's childhood home. I didn't expect her to have lived this close to the beach. Knowing that these houses are probably millions of dollars makes my throat feel tight. I do well for myself, but not *this* well.

"These houses are amazing," I comment as we make our final turn.

"They're beautiful," she says, and I hear the sadness in her voice. Even without knowing all of the memories attached to the house, I can understand her sadness. I wouldn't want to lose a place like this either.

We pull into the driveway of a pale blue beach house next to two other cars. A man leads a toddler out of the front door, holding his hand. When he looks up, his eyebrows raise.

"Is now a good time to mention I didn't tell my family you were coming?" Zara asks and I whip my head toward her.

"What?" I feel panic begin to rise within me. "Why didn't you tell them? Why didn't you tell *me*?" I try to keep calm, but it's difficult. Zara and I don't have an official relationship title. How do I introduce myself? *Hi, I'm Brad, Zara's kind of boss who decided to tag along on her five-hour road trip to see her family during a deeply personal time.* Nope, don't like that.

"I didn't know how to tell either of you. I panicked, and I'm sorry, but if we stay in here any longer my brother is going to come and knock on your window, so we have to pull ourselves together now," she says quickly, then pushes open the car door and plasters on a smile. I take a deep breath and get out as well.

"Hey, Drake," Zara says, then crouches down in front of the young boy. "Hey, sweet boy," she coos and pulls him into her arms. The sight makes me smile.

"Glad to see you love your nephew more than your own brother," Drake jokes as she rises to her feet and steps into his arms.

She laughs. "He has tiny hands and chubby cheeks, of course I love him more."

"Are you going to introduce me?" Drake asks once they pull apart. Zara pulls down her hoodie sleeves and looks over her shoulder at me with a shy smile.

"Drake, this is my friend Brad; Brad, this is my brother Drake and his son Liam." She ruffles Liam's wispy blonde hair.

I clear my throat and step forward. "It's nice to meet you," I say and hold out my hand to Drake. He grips it firmly and shakes it.

"Same to you. How do you know Zara?" he asks, and I can sense him sizing me up.

"We work together," I respond, and he gives a slow, skeptical nod.

"I thought I'd heard her mention a Brad before. Well, I hope you came ready to work. Our mom is practically a hoarder and half of her stuff is weird antique pieces that are made of solid wood."

I laugh at his description.

"I'm ready. I told Zara I'd help however I could," I say, and he looks between Zara and me.

"You're a good friend," he says, but the way he says friend sounds more like a question than a statement. Zara picks up Liam and takes a step toward the house.

"Let's go inside, it's too cold and wet out here for little Liam." Zara smiles nervously.

"I brought him out here to get out from under everyone else, but now that you're here you can entertain him," Drake says with a smirk.

We walk up the white porch steps and in through the matching door. The inside is just as nice as the outside, with pale wood floors and an open floor plan. The openness is to my detriment, though, because everyone currently in the kitchen can now see us coming in the door. Conversation has halted and I feel as though I've stepped on stage under a spotlight and forgotten all my lines.

"Mom's name is Diane. Don't call her Mrs. Thomas. You can do this," Drake says and gives me a hard slap on the back. "Zara brought some extra muscles for us. Now I won't have to lift the hutch all by myself," he yells out and chuckles.

I walk beside Zara into the kitchen where two women stand together, one with a baby snuggled against her chest. Zara hugs the woman with the baby first, then pauses in front of the other.

"Hi, mom," she says quietly. Her mother imme-diately pulls her into a hug. Zara hesitates for a moment before slowly wrapping her arms around her in a hug.

"Thank goodness you're here. Your brother doesn't know how to wrap up my teacups and it's driving me crazy!" I stifle a laugh at Diane's over-the-top tone. Her eyes flick up to me and I put on a polite smile. "Who's this?"

"I'm Brad, a friend of Zara's. It's nice to meet you, Diane," I say, and she raises her thin eyebrows slightly.

"A *friend*. I see." She purses her lips together. "I'm glad my daughter has such helpful friends." What is with this family and their strange tones surrounding the word friend? I know it's odd for me to be here, but still. Give a guy a break.

I glance down at Zara to find her toying with the string of her hoodie. She looks up at me, lifts a shoulder, and gives me a 'what can you do?' smile. It breaks up any anxiety hiding within me. I can do this. I can make it through an awkward few days, and maybe by the end of it, I'll get to say I'm more than just a *friend*.

CHAPTER 17

Zara Thomas

"Your friend is pretty cute," Annabeth, my sister-in-law, giggles from beside me. We're currently hand-wrapping all of my mother's glass turtles. Yes—glass turtle figurines. She started collecting them after Drake was born and hasn't stopped. They have their own cabinet.

"Cute? What are you, twelve?" I bump her shoulder lightly, but she only laughs more.

"I'm twenty-seven and I know an attractive man when I see one." She wiggles her eyebrows, making me roll my eyes.

"So now he's attractive?" I fold tissue paper over the delicate turtle figurine's head–this one has a top hat.

"Who's attractive?" Brad's deep voice makes me jump, and I almost drop a turtle.

"Nobody!" I say at the same time Annabeth says, "Bradley Cooper!"

Brad raises an eyebrow and I cut my eyes to Annabeth. She pastes on a less than innocent smile.

"We were talking about how you share the same name as Bradley Cooper," I lie and he grins, crossing his arms and leaning against the doorframe. I find myself taking him in. He's shed his flannel and now has on a white V-neck. The shirt clings to his chest slightly due to him sweating while carrying all of the heavy furniture, and I quickly avert my gaze. Friends do *not* check friends out.

"Is that so? Well I can leave you to talk about celebrity crushes, but Drake was talking about getting some food."

"Thank goodness, I'm starving!" Annabeth says and sets down the turtle she was wrapping. "I'm going to make sure my son doesn't look like a gremlin before we go out in public." She laughs as she walks out of the room. Brad moves to let her pass then turns to me again.

"While we're alone..." He pauses and my skin flames thinking of all the implications of that tiny phrase. But the look Brad gives me isn't flirty; instead his brow furrows in concern. "Are you okay? How have you been?"

My shoulders sag and I sigh. "I've been better. Being around Annabeth has helped, but it's still difficult."

"Do you want to talk about it?" I can't face the sincerity in his eyes, so I turn back to the glass figures and try to busy myself. There's still at least a hundred more to individually wrap.

"I don't know what to say. I'm packing up my childhood home, which sucks. But that's all."

"At the risk of sounding like a cheesy therapist from a sitcom: How does that make you feel?" I laugh at his description then shrug.

"Sad, I guess. I hate knowing that I'll never get to come back here. I won't get to spend Christmas here, which was my favorite. I won't get to bring my kids here. At least Drake got to bring Liam."

"And what about things with your parents? How's that?"

I place another figure in the storage tote. I suddenly have the urge to break one. Or the whole box. "Frustrating. My mom hasn't said a word. She's pretending like it's all normal. My dad doesn't say much on the phone, just that he's sad he won't see us for Thanksgiving."

"That's awful, Z. I'm sorry that this is happening to you. I'll be here for you the next few days and after we get back to Atlanta. You can vent to me, or we can go and do something to get your mind off it. I'd even be willing to watch that awful show you love so much."

I laugh as my heart skips in my chest. It's hard to believe he'd be willing to do all of this for me, but at the same time I know he's genuine.

I turn around to face him, but he's closer than I thought, forcing me to look up at him.

"Thank you," I whisper.

"Anything to see that smile of yours again," he replies, and my lips automatically form a small smile.

Our eyes lock. His are a dreamy pastel blue today, reminiscent of the ocean at sunrise. I feel as if I'm lost at sea, and yet also the safest I've ever been. His eyelashes flutter down as his gaze shifts to my lips briefly then back up to my eyes. He takes a half-step forward and without thinking I match it. Like the tide to the shore, I can't help but be drawn in.

Another half-step and my heart picks up speed in my chest. I close the distance between our feet. We're standing toe-to-toe. He runs a hand up my arm and over my shoulder—

"Zara!" I jump away from Brad and knock my back into the table. All of the turtles wobble in sync like some sort of odd dance, but thankfully none of them fall.

"Are you okay?" The heat in Brad's gaze is replaced by concern. Before I can answer him, my mother enters the room.

"Zara, are you coming? The diner is the only place in town open the day before Thanksgiving and we won't be able to get a table together if you keep wasting time!" she chastises, making me sigh. My entire childhood is crumbling but yes, let's worry about a table for dinner.

"Yes, Mom, I'm coming. We'll find a table just fine," I assure her, and she gives a curt nod before turning on her heel.

"We still need to move quickly!" she says over her shoulder as she leaves the room. I feel Brad's gaze on me the whole time.

"Z?" Brad checks on me again, and I avoid his eyes.

"I'm okay," I tell him. But I'm far from it. I feel like I was drowning, and I just came up for air. My breathing is shallow, and I can't get a handle on what just happened.

I think...I think I'm falling for Brad.

CHAPTER 18

Brad Jennings

I groan as I roll over on the air mattress I slept on last night. Though I didn't really sleep, mostly tossed and turned on the plastic torture device while it slowly deflated. I glare at the air pump plugged into the wall. Halfway through the night I wanted to get up and inflate the mattress again, but I was afraid to wake Zara's family up. I might as well have slept on a plastic tarp.

I grab my phone off Drake's office floor–where I was placed since I came unannounced–and check the time. It's not even eight in the morning and I'm already dreading another night of this, but it's worth it if I can help Zara. She seemed lighter after our conversation yesterday, just a bit shy. Considering how close we were to kissing though, that checks out.

I push up off the air mattress and then rub my hands over my face as I think. I wish I could have gone back in time and had the guts to tell her how I felt earlier. Then maybe I'd be her boyfriend on this trip and not second-guessing every lingering look or almost kiss. I can't push her. I don't *want* to push her. But I'm going crazy not knowing where we stand. Hopefully, once we're back in Atlanta, we can figure things out. For now, I need to be here for Zara as a friend.

This is increasingly difficult though, because she keeps looking up at me with eyes that scream *kiss me!* But I can be strong. I have willpower. I just have to muster it up each time I see her.

I open the office door to the scent of sage and garlic. My stomach growls and I follow the smell to the kitchen. Annabeth is stirring something on the stove while Drake sits with Liam as he eats what looks to be a toddler-sized pancake.

"Morning, Brad!" Annabeth chirps when she spots me standing in the archway.

"Good morning. Is Zara up yet?" As welcoming as Annabeth and Drake have been, it still feels odd to hang out with Zara's family without her.

"She's down at the beach," Drake says as he places a few more pancake pieces on Liam's high chair tray. "If I had to bet, she probably lost track of time. When I got up there was a note on the counter saying she'd be back later. If you take a left out the front door there's a beach entrance not far. Shouldn't be too hard to spot her this early." It's barely eight in the morning, so Zara must not have slept well either if she was gone before everyone got up.

"Thanks, I'll go check on her," I say. He shares a look with Annabeth that I don't want to think about too much.

"I've been preparing for dinner tonight, so the stove and oven are taken up, but we have muffins and frozen pancakes if you want breakfast when you get back," Annabeth says, and I smile. After thanking them both again, I quickly leave the house.

The morning air is salty and feels cool on my skin. If I wasn't in a hurry to check on Zara, I'd take this walk slow and savor the breeze and take in the architecture. My mind is so set on her though, that the neighborhood becomes a pastel blur in my peripheral. I don't think she could be hurt or in too much distress, but I know being alone with all of those thoughts isn't always the best.

The beach is empty and–like Drake said–it's easy to spot Zara. Her blue hair is wild and wavy this morning with the wind tossing it in the air. She looks like a mermaid who just washed up on the shore.

I'm currently barefoot, so I go ahead and trudge through the cold sand down to her. The waves are louder as I get closer, and I can taste the salt spray on my lips.

"Z!" I raise my voice over the waves, and she whips around. Her eyes are rimmed red, and her face looks damp. She scrambles to her feet as I walk over.

"Hey," she chokes out and wipes at her face with the sleeve of her oversized sweatshirt. "I must have lost track of time. I didn't mean to leave you alone with my family."

"Don't worry about it, it's no big deal. I just came to check on you. Drake said you've been out here for a few hours." I step closer to her. We're almost as close as we were yesterday in her childhood home.

"I'm okay, I just wanted to be alone, away from the tension that keeps rising in my family. It's suffocating." She wraps her arms around herself.

"Did I interrupt? I can go back and tell everyone you'll be here for a while. I'll guard the beach entrance," I say.

She smiles, but it's faint.

"No, it's okay." Her voice is quiet, and I can't tell if she's trying to appease me or not.

"You don't have to say that, Z. It's alright. I'll go so you can be alone," I say with a reassuring smile. I take a step back and her hand reaches out, grabbing mine.

"No, really! I'd rather you be here." I glance down at our hands then back at her.

"Are you just saying that because it's me?" I don't want her to feel like she has to entertain me. I can handle some awkward small talk with her family if need be.

"Yes," she says with a light laugh that lifts my concern some. "I'm saying it because I want you to stay here with me. If you were someone else, I'd tell you to go."

I can't contain the goofy grin that crosses my face even if I wanted to. If someone walked up to me and told me the Braves' had just won the World Series, it still wouldn't beat hearing that Zara wants *me* to stay with her. No one else. *Me.* "Then I'll stay."

She lets go of my hand and I stifle a frown. "Good. Now let me show you where I spent ninety percent of my time as a child," she says with a wistful smile that makes my heart ache. I want nothing more than to make this problem go away for her, but I can't. We're packing the house up more today before dinner, and tomorrow we leave.

An idea comes to me as Zara recounts how she snuck out to the beach on Christmas Eve one year, hoping to spot Santa in the night sky. I can't give Zara her house back, but maybe I can give her one last good memory to hold onto when it's gone...

CHAPTER 19

Zara Thomas

Today was less painful than I thought it would be. After Brad came to the beach, I spent the rest of the day laughing and smiling. That seems to be the theme of anything involving Brad. Even when my mom made a comment about the house being sold because of my dad, I was still able to smile through it with one caring look from him.

But now the day is over, and Brad is already in bed. He said he didn't sleep well last night and needed to rest up before the drive tomorrow. So now I'm alone with my thoughts and a half-eaten piece of pumpkin pie. My dad usually makes the pie, but this one is store-bought. It's not bad, but it's no comparison.

"You gonna eat that pie or just stare at it?" Drake says as he walks into the kitchen. He's carrying a

Paw Patrol sippy cup, probably getting it ready for Liam for after his bath. I shrug and run my fork over the mostly melted whip cream while he fills the sippy cup with milk.

"I know I won't be able to sleep. Too much on my mind. Maybe I'll go back to the beach. Do you have a big flashlight I can use?"

He screws on the cap and then puts the milk back in the fridge. "I have a better idea. Why don't you go down to the house? You can see it one last time while no one's there and get to say goodbye alone."

I purse my lips, thinking over his suggestion. It would be nice to be there alone. No one grunting while they move heavy furniture or criticizing my packing skills.

"That sounds like a good idea, actually. Thanks, Drake," I say with a smile.

"Keys are on the hook by the door. Don't stay out too late." His smile seems a tad mischievous, but I brush it off. I haven't slept much, so I could be misinterpreting things.

My parents' house, or rather what used to be their house, is just two roads away from Drake's. I make the walk using my phone flashlight. When I get there, I see Brad's car out front, and it looks like some lights are on inside. The last time I saw Brad's car, it was in Drake's driveway. He had driven over the last load of small boxes in his backseat. It shouldn't be here unless...unless Brad's here.

My heart is beating out of my chest as I turn the doorknob. I gasp as soon as I enter. Twinkle lights hang from the ceiling, casting a warm glow on the living room. In the middle of the mostly empty space is a Christmas tree, strung with lights and covered in red and gold ornaments that look so much like the ones from my childhood he must have gotten them from my mom's Christmas boxes.

There's a blanket on the ground by the tree with pillows strewn about and a laptop open as well with a fireplace filling the screen. It even smells like Christmas, with notes of cinnamon and pine in the air. And next to it all is Brad, looking nervous and handsome in his flannel pajamas.

"Bradley Jennings," I whisper as tears well up in my eyes. Never in my life have I felt so *seen*, so *cared for*.

"You used my full name. So either you're mad or you really like it." He laughs, but I can tell he's nervous.

"I love it. This is the sweetest thing anyone has ever done for me."

He crosses the room with a smile on his face. "I wanted you to have one last Christmas here. We can watch a Christmas movie together and I found some Oreos in Drake's pantry. They aren't Christmas cookies but—"

I grab his pajama shirt and pull him down into a kiss.

He stays frozen for just a moment, like a buffering sign before a movie plays. But once he makes a move, the wait is well worth it. One hand wraps around my waist while the other slides under my jaw. I feel every ounce of yearning and hope in each brush of his lips, each gentle caress of his thumb on my cheek. His fingers press into the dip of my waist, and he pulls me in closer like he's desperate for more, but our kiss never quickens. It stays slow, like I'm the very last dessert on earth and he wants to savor me.

When our lips finally part, he doesn't create any distance between us. Instead, he presses a featherlight kiss to the corner of my mouth, sending shivers down my spine. Then he smiles against my lips, and I know I'm ruined for life. There's no way any man can kiss me like he just did, I'm convinced.

"I've wanted to do that for a very long time," he whispers, his breath fanning my face.

"Did it live up to your expectations?" I joke, because I can barely think of anything beyond wanting to kiss him again.

He presses another sweet, lingering kiss on my lips. It leaves me breathless. "Does that answer your question?" He murmurs in a husky voice, and I merely nod.

When he takes a step back, I have to resist the urge to pull him to me again. "I don't want to be selfish and take you away from this last memory in your childhood home. Do you want to watch a movie together?" he asks, and I smile up at him.

"As long as there's more kissing in our future," I say, and he chuckles before giving me a heated look.

"Our future looks very promising in that area." I blush and make my way over to the blanket. We sit down together and Brad kisses the crown of my head after wrapping an arm around my shoulders.

"What movie should we watch?" he asks as he exits out of the fireplace ambiance video he had on.

"How about *Claymation Rudolph*?" I ask, and he turns to look at me, a wide grin on his face.

"If you keep being so perfect, Zara Thomas, I'm going to have to marry you," he jokes.

A girl can hope.

Epilogue

Zara Thomas

Three weeks later

"Are you nervous?" I ask as I tug on the strings of my hoodie. Brad stands up from his desk chair and stretches before giving me a heart-stopping smile. The very smile that's made me fall in love with him more and more each day. I haven't exactly told him yet, but I will. I'm just waiting on the right time. He hasn't told me yet, but I feel like he's just trying not to scare me. Considering he told me he was falling for me a while ago, it seems more likely than not.

I know that he's worried about moving too fast with me after my parent's divorce, too. It hasn't been easy adjusting to a new family dynamic. I've already had to plan out my Christmas vacation so that I can see both my mom and my dad at their respective houses. I never thought I'd have to worry about things like this. But Brad being with me through it all has been the best. I've felt taken care of always, and he always manages to cheer me up after a wayward phone call with my mom. He's an amazing boyfriend, which is why I feel like I'm ready to take the next step.

"Why would I be nervous? Callum is one of my best friends, and you're one of Charlotte's. They should be happy for us."

"That's true," I say and bite my lip. I don't think they'll be mad, except Charlotte. She'll be mad that I didn't tell her sooner. But keeping things private has been nice. Sneaking around isn't half bad either. Secret breakroom kisses…that's all I'm going to say.

"You seem nervous, though. You were nervous last night too. Are you not ready to tell him?" I sigh and tuck my hands in the pocket of my hoodie. Last night I almost told him I loved him after we watched a movie together. It was on the tip of my tongue, until Charlotte called asking if my brides-maid dress came in. Then I felt like the moment had gone.

Now it's time to tell Callum so we can then go to HR, but I feel like I'm holding our relationship back by not telling him. At the same time, telling him I love him in a cubicle wasn't exactly what I'd imagined.

"I'm not nervous about telling Callum or Charlotte," I say to start, but I can't get any other words out. I look down at my bright white tennis shoes, focusing on them instead of him.

"Is something wrong?" Fingertips brush under my chin, lifting my head up to meet my favorite light blue eyes. Even under these awful fluorescents they're beautiful. They've started to look like home to me.

"Nothing's wrong, I've just been meaning to tell you something," I say, and he tugs me into his arms.

"You can tell me anything, Z." There's a tinge of worry in his voice and I hate that I'm the cause of it.

"I love you," I blurt out while staring at the top button of his flannel. I cringe at my delivery and peek up at him to see his reaction. The warmth in his gaze floors me. I've never had anyone look at me with such pure adoration and happiness before.

He dips his head and kisses me softly. "I love you too, Zara," he whispers against my lips before capturing them in another bone-melting kiss.

Someone clears their throat from behind us and we jump apart. I spin around, almost falling from the dizzying kiss, and see Callum with his eyebrows raised.

"I'm guessing this is the news y'all were coming to share?" His face betrays no emotion. I can't tell whether he's ecstatic or furious.

"Yes." Brad clears his throat. "We wanted to tell you before we went to HR. Sorry you found out this way." I look over at him and stifle a giggle at his mussed hair and red-tinged cheeks. I'm sure I look similar.

"It's about time!" Callum surprises me with a good-natured chuckle. "Everyone has been saying you two were going to get together since the bachelor party."

My mouth drops open.

"People have been talking about us?" I squeak out and Callum laughs again.

"Yeah, we've been rooting for y'all this whole time. I thought after your trip to Charleston you'd come back dating, but I guess you needed more time."

I look down at my feet to hide my smile.

"Well, actually," Brad laughs. "We started dating in Charleston, but we kept it a secret."

"Man, I lost five dollars!"

"You *bet* on us?" I ask, giving him an incredulous look.

"Everyone did! I'm going to get my money back from MJ and Bennett. They said it would take longer, but I knew that trip would be the catalyst."

I shake my head at him, laughing.

"I guess you were right," Brad says with a smile that I match.

"Charlotte was so disappointed when you came back not dating. She'll be half-excited, half-furious when you tell her the truth," Callum says, and I laugh again. That sounds about right. "Well, I'm happy for you both, really. Now get back to work. If someone else catches you kissing in here again I don't want to deal with the HR report."

He walks away, and Brad draws me into his arms once more.

"Didn't you hear him? We need to get back to work." I giggle.

"I heard him say if someone catches us. So we'll just have to be more covert," he says huskily then leans down to kiss me again. I melt into his arms, the happiest I've ever been. I could stay here for-ever...and I just might.

Curious about how Charlotte and Callum met? Be sure to read their enemies to lovers, grumpy/sunshine romcom The Love Audit!

Author's Note

Hello darling reader!

I'm so glad you're here, because that means (hopefully haha) you finished this novella! So thank you for living in the Sweet Peach Series world for a little while. This short and sweet book came to be because so many of you asked about Zara getting her own book. And some of you already had her paired with Brad after their friendship in my first book The Love Audit.

If you haven't read any of my previous books, then you should go back and see how these two have known each other and get glimpses of their characters throughout the series! All of my books are standalones, but I think they're best read in order because you get to see the characters develop in ways you won't by reading just one.

No matter if you read this book in order of the series or not, I hope you enjoyed it and you'll stick around for future books. Personally, this might be the most fun I've had thus far writing a book, haha! Low angst, just fun for this one. I wanted these two to have a sweet story that showed their characters but wasn't overly complicated or intense.

I know some of you might be wishing the book was longer, but a novella made the most sense to me for these two lovebirds! In the future you can look forward to seeing some cameos in the rest of the series as well as some bonus chapters from their POV.

If you loved it, feel free to check out my other books. You can find all the info you need on my website: annahconwell.com

Also, PLEASE come find me on social media so we can chat! Any of my readers will tell you I'm so down to hear your reactions. Give me all the details!

Instagram: @authorannahconwell

Facebook Reader Group: Annah's Book Babes

Acknowledgments

Jesus, everything good in me is from You. Thank you.

As always, thank you to my husband Ryan for your unwavering support and hilarious commentary on my books. You might have loved Brad and Zara more than me, LOL! I couldn't do any of this without you. I love you!

Thank you to Dulcie Dameron, my critique partner and sweet friend. You get the messy so everyone else can get the great. And yet you still love my characters and work just as much if not more than those who get the finished product. You're an amazing author, woman, and friend!

Thank you to my booksta besties, my sisters in Christ: Baylie, Kathryn, and Bethany. Y'all make me laugh so hard I cry, and make me actually cry with your support of my work. Whenever I'm feeling less than as an author, you lift me up and encourage me.

Special thanks to my friends and family and community who have supported me by buying books, sharing on social media, and talking about them. You're the best!

Shoutout to my newsletter book babes for your sweet emails and excitement about the book. I love y'all!

To my editor, Caitlin Miller, thank you for going with the flow on fast releases. And for loving my characters and being so kind to me.

To my cover designer, Stephanie, sometimes I put you through the wringer I feel like, LOL! When I said I didn't know what to put on this cover, you made it happen. You're a gem and a dang good designer. Thank you for being you!

Lastly, thank YOU wonderful reader, for spending time in these pages and letting me live out my dream.

About Author

Annah Conwell is a sweet romcom author who loves witty banter, sassy heroines, and swoony heroes. She has a passion for writing books that make you LOL one minute and melt into a puddle of 'aw' the next. You can find her living out her days in a small town in Sweet Home Alabama (roll tide roll!) with the love of her life (aka her husband), Ryan, and her two goofball pups, Prince and Ella.

She loves coffee, the color pink, and playing music way too loud in the car. Most of the time she's snuggled up under her favorite blanket on the couch, reading way too many books to call it anything other than an addiction, or writing her little hopeless romantic heart out.

Made in the USA
Coppell, TX
25 September 2024

37724101R00069